To old friends and new friends

Atheneum Books for Young Readers
An imprint of Simon & Schuster Children's Publishing Division
1230 Avenue of the Americas
New York, New York 10020

Book design by Ann Bobco
The text of this book is set in Deepdene.
The illustrations are rendered in watercolor.

First Edition
Printed in Hong Kong
10 9 8 7 6 5 4 3 2 1

Library of Congress Cataloging-in-Publication Data
Mathers, Petra.
Lottie's new friend / by Petra Mathers.—1st ed.
p. cm.
"An Anne Schwartz book."
Summary: When a new bird moves in nearby, Herbie the duck worries that his friend Lottie the chicken doesn't care about him anymore.
ISBN 0-689-82014-3 (alk. paper)
[1. Friendship—Fiction. 2. Birds—Fiction.]
I. Title. PZ7.M42475Lo 1999
[E]—dc21 98-21625

Lottie's New Friend

by petra mathers

An Anne Schwartz Book
ATHENEUM BOOKS FOR YOUNG READERS

Every day, rain or shine, Herbie went to see his best friend, Lottie.

"Li-la-Lottie, I smell cookies in the oven, nice and hottie.

Hm, I wonder who's here?"

"There you are," said Lottie. "Herbie, this is our new neighbor Dodo from Germany. She's fixing up Bufflehead's old place."

"Oh," said Herbie. "I brought you some flowers, Lottie."

"Thank you, dear. They'll look pretty with Dodo's bunch.

"Just think, Herbie, Dodo was in the movies," said Lottie.

"Only once," said Dodo, "and it wos a verry smoll part."

Lottie and Dodo talked and talked.
Herbie ate one cookie after another.

He played with his lemonade . . .

. . . until it went down the wrong pipe.
"Ach, ze poor duck," said Dodo.

Herbie still had the hiccups on his way
home. "How much does Lottie . . . hic . . .
really like me?" he wondered.

The next morning Herbie called and invited
Lottie for a boat ride. "Lovely," she said.
"Dodo is here, we'll meet you at the dune."

Maybe Dodo will get seasick, Herbie
thought.

"I like a nice boat drive," said Dodo.
"Dodo's father is a captain, Herbie," said Lottie.
I'm the captain here, thought Herbie and revved up the engine.

Suddenly they hit a rock.
"SOS!" shouted Herbie.

The cotter pin was broken.
"Use zis hairpin, Herbie," said Dodo.
"It is a trick I know."

On the way back Herbie felt very small. Lottie and Dodo didn't notice.

The next day Dodo was just leaving
Lottie's when Herbie arrived. "Doesn't she
look smart in her new glasses?" Lottie said.

I bet no one would care if I went blind,
Herbie thought going home.

I bet no one would care if I were dead,
he thought going to bed.

Herbie was having a beautiful dream when
the phone rang.

"Aunt Mattie is sick. I'm leaving on the next bus," said Lottie.
"I'll take you to the station," said Herbie.

"What's wrong with Aunt Mattie?" asked Herbie.
"Stones in her gizzard," said Lottie.
"Ouch," said Herbie.

"Good-bye Lottie, come back soon."

The days crept by. Without Lottie *The Perils of Mr. Pea* seemed boring.

Herbie went down to the dock to practice his knots, but his heart wasn't in it. Maybe the mail had come?

Nothing, not even way back.

"I guess I could go see how Dodo's fixing up old Bufflehead's place."

Herbie wasn't sure if he wanted to talk to Dodo, so he put on his disguise.

Is that Dodo on the roof? he wondered. Something looked wrong. Herbie started to run.

Dodo had been overcome by her fear of heights.
"Heaven above, help me down," she sobbed.

"Hold on, mate, I'm coming up," a voice
  shouted.

"Herbie," cried Dodo, "you are an angel!"

Getting off the ladder, Dodo's legs wobbled. "What you need is a nice hot bath," said Herbie.

With Dodo safe, Herbie headed home. "Now I know . . ." Dodo called after him,

". . . why Lottie says, 'You can always count on Herbie.'"
"She does?" said Herbie.

"Yes, and zat you are ze apple of her eye."

Dear Herbie,
Aunt Mattie on the
mend. I'll be on
the 5 o'clock. Can't
wait to see you.
Love, Lottie

POST CARD

Herbie
Crookroad
Oysterville

20 USA

Malus pumila

At home Herbie found a postcard.
He called Dodo.

"Guess who's coming home tomorrow?"
he said. "I'm making gingersnaps with
leaf loaf. We'll have a party!"

They got to the station early. They didn't mind. It was nice, waiting together.

When the bus pulled in, Lottie was first to get off. "Oh my," she said, "am I glad to see you."